# THE 100-POUND PROBLEM

by Jennifer Dussling
Illustrated by Rebecca Thornburgh

The Kane Press
New York

Book Design/Art Direction: Roberta Pressel

Library of Congress Cataloging-in-Publication Data

Dussling, Jennifer.
    The 100-pound problem/by Jennifer Dussling; illustrated by Rebecca Thornburgh.
      p.   cm. — (Math matters.)
    Summary: Before he can go fishing, a boy has to figure out how to get himself, his dog
  and all his gear out to an island in a boat that can only carry 100 pounds.
      ISBN 1-57565-095-9 (pbk.  :  alk. paper)
    [1. Weights and measures—Fiction.  2. Boats and boating—Fiction.] I. Title: One-hundred-
  pound problem. II. Thornburgh, Rebecca McKillip, ill. III. Title. IV. Series.
  PZ7.D943 Aaj   2000
  [E]—dc21                                                           99-42679
                                                                         CIP
                                                                          AC

10  9  8  7  6  5  4  3  2  1

First published in the United States of America in 2000 by The Kane Press.
Printed in Hong Kong.

MATH MATTERS is a registered trademark of The Kane Press.

It was a bright sunny day. A no-school day.
A perfect day for fishing. And that's just what
Walt was going to do.

People were fishing on shore. They hadn't caught much. But that didn't bother Walt. He was going to the island—thanks to his cousin Roger.

Roger said Walt could borrow his
boat. He didn't let just anybody use it.
His dad had made it, and it was special.

BOATING RULES
- Don't overload the boat.
- Wear life vest.
- If storm comes up, head for shore.
~Water Safety Council~

Walt put down his stuff. Right away his dog Patch started nosing the lunch bag. It was those roast beef sandwiches! "No, Patch!" Walt said. Patch looked guilty.

Walt turned the boat over. There was writing on it.

This boat holds only 100 pounds. -Roger

"Uh-oh," Walt said to Patch. "I bet we have more than 100 pounds!"

Walt knew he weighed about 65 pounds.
The school nurse had told him so. He knew
Patch weighed 20 pounds. That's what the
vet had said. That was 85 pounds right there!

Then there was all his stuff. His lunch.
His fishing gear. His heavy backpack. What
did all that weigh?

"Too bad we don't have a scale, huh, Patch?"
Walt said.

Then it came to him. He could make a scale!

Walt found a plank from an old boat. He balanced it over a rock. It looked a little like a seesaw.

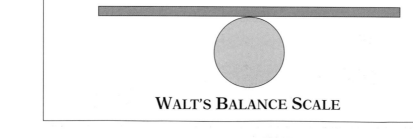

**WALT'S BALANCE SCALE**

"Okay, Patch," Walt said. "You're going to help me."

Walt pointed to his scale. Patch jumped on.

"Now I can find out what my stuff weighs compared to you," Walt explained.

Gently Walt put the backpack on the scale. The scale did not move. That meant the backpack weighed less than Patch.

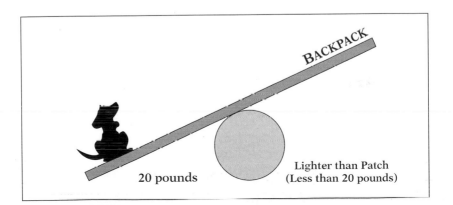

BACKPACK

20 pounds

Lighter than Patch
(Less than 20 pounds)

"Now I'll weigh the fishing gear," said Walt.

The scale still did not move. So the gear was lighter than Patch, too.

"You know what?" Walt said. "I'm putting ALL my stuff on the scale!"

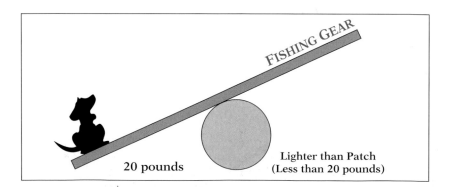

FISHING GEAR

20 pounds

Lighter than Patch
(Less than 20 pounds)

He did—and Patch's end swung up!
Now Walt knew that all three things
together were heavier than Patch.

20 pounds        Heavier than Patch!
                 (More than 20 pounds)

"What if I take something away?" Walt wondered.

He told Patch to sit on the scale again. Then Walt took his lunch off.

The scale balanced!

"Amazing!" Walt said. "That means the fishing gear plus the backpack weigh 20 pounds—the same as you, Patch!"

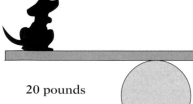

20 pounds

FISHING GEAR
BACKPACK

Same as Patch!
(20 pounds)

"Now I know what to do," Walt said.
"I'll take just a few things at a time. And I'll
be careful not to have more than 100 pounds
in the boat."

15

For his first trip Walt took his lunch
and the fishing gear.

As he pushed off, Patch looked at Walt
with sad eyes. "Sorry, boy," Walt said. "If I
take you too, we'll be over 100 pounds.
You can go next time."

HAPPY BIRTHDAY, DANA!

The boat skimmed across the bay.
Off to one side, a bird snapped a big
fish right out of the water!

"I hope I'll be as lucky as that bird,"
Walt thought.

at holds
0 pounds.
Roger

It took Walt only a few minutes to row his
gear and his lunch to the island and back
to shore. Patch was waiting. "Get in, boy!"
Walt said.

Walt looked at his backpack. "I'm not exactly
sure how much the backpack weighs," he
thought. "I'll play it safe and make another trip."

Patch loved the boat ride. Every time he saw another boat, he barked hello. One boat had a big dog in it. Patch got very excited. He barked and wagged his tail until the other dog barked back.

This boat holds only 100 pounds. —Roger

When Walt reached the island, Patch jumped out of the boat and ran right to the lunch bag. He sniffed it and whined.

"No, Patch!" Walt cried. It was the roast beef sandwiches. Patch *loved* roast beef.

"Uh-oh!" Walt thought. "I have to get my backpack. But I can't leave Patch alone here with my sandwiches. They'll be gone by the time I get back!"

"I know!" Walt said. The answer was easy. He could leave Patch on the island—and take the lunch bag in the boat with him! "I'll be back in no time," he told Patch.

When Walt got back from his third trip, Patch started jumping and barking. "Are you glad to see me, or is it the sandwiches?" Walt joked.

He pulled ashore and took a deep breath. Now he had everything just where he wanted it.

"Guess what, Patch?" Walt said. "It's time to go fishing!" Patch jumped in the boat.

Walt rowed out and cast the line into
the water. At last he was doing what he'd
set out to do—he was fishing. It felt great.

All of a sudden there was a tug on
Walt's line. A big tug! That meant a fish
had the bait. A big fish!

The pole bent like a bow, but Walt held on tight. The fish fought and fought. Patch barked and barked.

Finally Walt reeled the fish in.

It was a big fish… a heavy fish! Oh, no!
How could the boat hold Walt *and* Patch
*and* the fishing gear *and* the big, heavy
fish?

Before Walt could decide what to do…

SPLASH!
Patch had figured it out!

Patch swam to the island. He shook himself dry. And then, as Walt watched from the boat, Patch gave himself his own reward for being such a smart dog.

This boat holds only 100 pounds. - Roger

Walt didn't even mind. After all, he'd had a great day. He had caught a big fish, and he had solved the 100-pound problem. Could he have done it without Patch? No way!

# WEIGHT CHART

Look at Walt's balance scale. How does each weight compare to the mystery box?

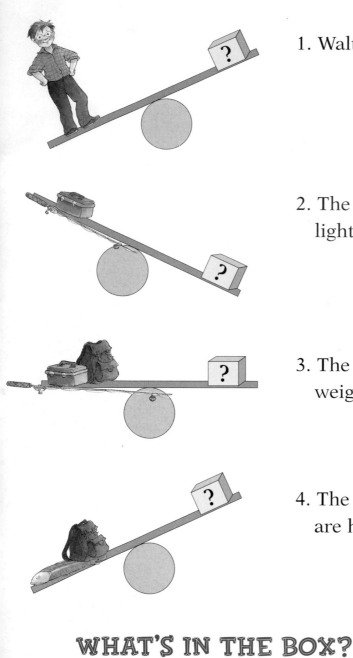

1. Walt is much heavier.

2. The fishing gear is lighter.

3. The backpack and gear weigh about the same.

4. The fish and backpack are heavier.

## WHAT'S IN THE BOX?